Text copyright © 1965 by Norton Juster.
Illustrations copyright © 1992 by Leonard Baskin.
Published by Picture Book Studio Ltd., Saxonville, Massachusetts.
Distributed in the United States by Simon & Schuster.
Distributed in Canada by Vanwell Publishing, St. Catharines, Ontario.
All rights reserved. Printed in Hong Kong.

Library of Congress Cataloging-in-Publication Data
Juster, Norton. 1929-
Alberic the Wise / written by Norton Juster ; illustrated by Leonard Baskin.
p. cm.
Summary: In the days of the Renaissance,
Alberic leads the reader among the folds of a rich tapestry in his search for wisdom.
ISBN 0-88708-243-2 : $19.95
[1. Wisdom—Fiction. 2. Renaissance—Fiction.]
I. Baskin, Leonard, 1922- ill. II. Title.
PZ7.J98Al   1992
[E]—dc20   92-7807
CIP
AC

NORTON JUSTER · LEONARD BASKIN

# ALBERIC
## the wise

Picture Book Studio

More than many years ago when fewer things had happened in the world and there was less to know, there lived a young man named Alberic who knew nothing at all. Well, almost nothing, or depending on your generosity of spirit, hardly anything, for he could hitch an ox and plow a furrow straight or thatch a roof or hone his scythe until the edge was bright and sharp or tell by a sniff of the breeze what the day would bring or with a glance when a grape was sweet and ready. But these were only the things he had to know to live or couldn't help knowing by living and are, as you may have discovered, rarely accounted as knowledge.

Of the world and its problems, however, he knew little, and indeed was even less aware of their existence. In all his life he had been nowhere and seen nothing beyond the remote estate on which he lived and to whose lands he and his family had been bound back beyond the edge of memory. He planted and harvested, threshed and winnowed, tended the hives and the pigs, breathed the country air, and stopped now and again to listen to the birds or puzzle at the wind. There were no mysteries, hopes or dreams other than those that could be encompassed by his often aching back or impatient stomach. This was the sum of his existence and with it he was neither happy nor sad. He simply could not conceive of anything else.

Since the days were much alike he measured his life by the more discernible seasons—yet they too slipped easily by, and would have continued to do so, I'm sure, had it not been for the lone traveler who appeared unaccountably one chill morning at the close of winter. Alberic watched him make his weary way along the road until, when they stood no more than a glance apart, he paused to rest before continuing on his journey. A curious old man—his tattered tunic was patched on patches and his worn shoes left hardly a suggestion of leather between himself and the cold ground. He carried a massive bundle on his back and sighed with the pleasure of letting it slide gently from his shoulder to the ground—then just as gently let himself down upon it. He nodded and smiled, mopped his face carefully with a handkerchief easily as old as himself, then acknowledged Alberic's timid greeting and finally began to speak, and when he did it was of many, many things.

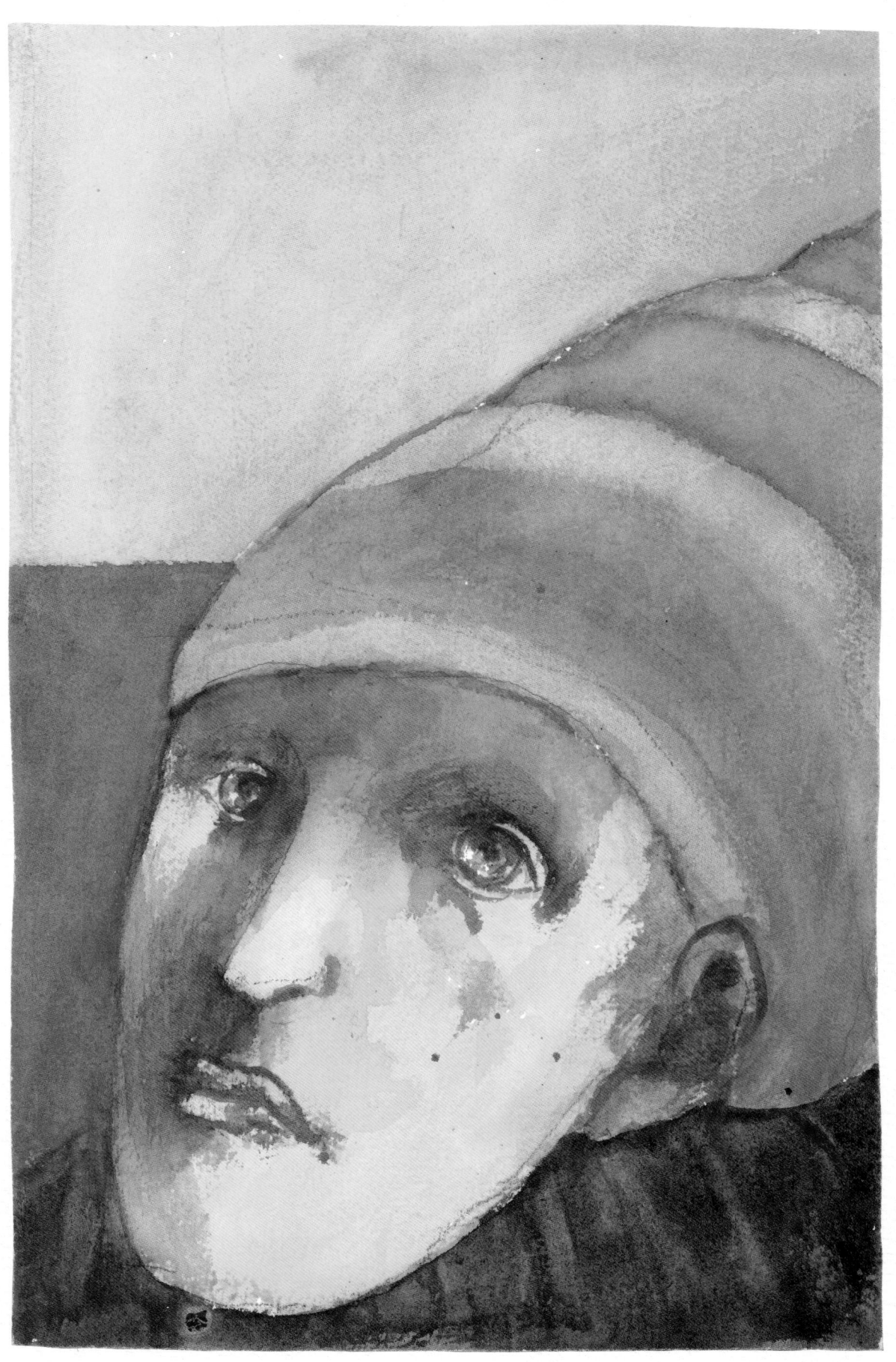

Where he had come from and where he was bound, what he had seen and what there was yet to discover—commonwealths, kingdoms, empires, counties and dukedoms—fortresses, bastions and great solitary castles that dug their fingers into the mountain passes and dared the world to pass—royal courts whose monarchs dressed in pheasant skins and silks and rich brocades of purple and lemon and crimson and bice all interlaced with figures of beasts and blossoms and strange geometric devices—and mountains that had no tops and oceans that had no bottoms.

There seemed no end to what he knew or what he cared to speak about, and speak he did, on and on through the day. His voice was soft and easy but his manner such that even his pauses commanded attention. And as he spoke his eyes sparkled and his words were like maps of unknown lands. He told of caravans that made their way across continents and back with perfumes and oils and dark red wines, sandalwood and lynx hides and ermine and carved sycamore chests, with cloves and cinnamon, precious stones and iron pots and ebony and amber and objects of pure tooled gold—of tall cathedral spires and cities full of life and craft and industry—of ships that sailed in every sea, and of art and science and learned speculation hardly even dreamed of by most people—and of armies and battles and magic and much, much more.

Alberic stood entranced, trying desperately to imagine all these wonderful things, but his mind could wander no further than the fields that he could see and the images soon would fade or cloud.

"The world is full of wonders," he sighed forlornly, for he realized that he could not even imagine what a wonder was.

"It is everything I've said and even more," the stranger replied, and since it was by now late afternoon he scrambled to his feet and once more took up his heavy bundle. "And remember," he said with a sweep of his arm, "it is all out there, just waiting." Then down the road and across the stubble fields he went.

For weeks after the old man had gone Alberic brooded, for now he knew that there were things he didn't know, and what magic and exciting things they were! Warm wet breezes had begun to blow across the land and the frozen fields had yielded first to mud and then to early blossoms. But now this quiet hillside was not enough to hold his rushing thoughts. "It is all out there, just waiting," he said to himself again and again, repeating the old man's words. When he had repeated them often enough, they became a decision. He secretly packed his few belongings and in the early morning's mist left his home and started down into the world to seek its wonders and its wisdom.

For two days and nights and half another day again he walked—through lonely forests and down along the rushing mountain streams that seemed to know their destination far better than he knew his. Mile after mile he walked until at last the trees and vines gave way to sweeps of easy meadowland and in the distance, barely visible, the towers of a city reflected back the sun's bright rays. As he approached, the hazy form became a jumble of roofs and chimney pots spread out below, and each step closer embellished them with windows, carved gables, domes and graceful spires. All this in turn was circled by a high wall which seemed to grow higher and wider as he descended towards it until at last it filled his vision and hid all else behind it. The stream which only days before had been so gay and playful now broadened and as if aware of its new importance assumed a slow and dignified pace as it passed through the city. Alberic paused for a moment to catch his breath, then, with a slight shiver of anticipation, passed beneath the cool dark gates and entered the city too.

What a teeming, busy place! Houses and shops, music and movement, all kinds of noises, signs and smells, and more people than he ever knew existed. He wandered along the cobbled streets delighted by each new discovery and noting with care the strange new sights and sounds so unfamiliar to his country senses. He soon learned too that he had come to a city famous above all others for the beautiful stained glass manufactured in its workshops.

"A noble and important profession," he decided soberly, "for surely beauty is the true aim of wisdom!" Without delay he went off to apprentice himself to the greatest of the master glassmakers.

"Well, well," growled the old craftsman after examining Alberic carefully, "so you want to make glass. Very well, we shall see. Your duties will be few and simple. Each morning you'll rise before the birds and with the other apprentices fetch sixty barrows of firewood from the forest. Then in each furnace bank a fire precisely hot enough to melt the lead and fuse the glass, and keep them tended constantly so that none goes out or varies even slightly in its heat. Then, of course, work the bellows, fetch the ingots from the foundry, run errands, assist the journeymen as they need, sharpen and repair all the chisels, files, knives, scrapers, shears, mallets and grozing irons so that each is in perfect order, make deliveries quickly and courteously, grind and mix the pigments, work the forge, sweep out the shop, fetch, carry, stoop, haul and bend, and in your spare time help with the household chores. You can of course eat your fill of the table scraps and sleep on the nice warm floor. Well, don't just stand there, you've only started and you're already hours behind in your work." When he finished he smiled a benevolent smile, for he was known for his generous nature.

Alberic applied himself to his new tasks with diligence, working from early morning until late at night when he would curl up in one corner of the shop to dream happily of the day's accomplishments and carefully sort and pack into his memory everything he'd learned. For some time he did only the menial jobs, but soon under the watchful eye of the master he began taking part in more important and exacting procedures. He learned to chip and shape the glass into pieces often no larger than the palm of his hand and then apply the colors mixed in gum or oil with a delicate badger brush and fire these to permanence in the glowing kilns. Then from measurements and patterns he learned to set each piece in the grooved strips of lead and solder them carefully at each joint. For almost two years he worked and watched as all these small and painstaking operations took form in great windows and medallions of saintly lives or tales of moral instruction which glowed in deep splendid blues and vivid rubies.

Finally the time came for Alberic to prove his skill and take his place among the glassmakers—to create a work entirely on his own. He was determined that it would be a rare and lovely thing and he set about it with quiet intensity.

"What will it be, Alberic?" they all asked eagerly.

"Beautiful," he replied with never a moment's doubt, and that was all he'd say.

And for weeks he worked secretly in one corner of the shop until the day came when his work was to be judged. Everyone gathered to see it. The master looked long and carefully. He stood back to view it in the light and squinted close at matters of fine detail, and then he rubbed his chin and then he tapped his finger and then he swayed and then he sighed and then he frowned.

"No," he said sadly and slowly, "certainly not. You will never be a glassmaker." And everyone agreed, for despite the best of intentions Alberic's work was poor indeed.

How miserable he was! How thoroughly miserable ! Why wasn't it beautiful when he had tried so hard? How could he have learned so much and yet still fail? No one knew the answer. "There is no reason now for me to stay," he said quietly, gathering up his bundle, and without even as much as a last look back he walked out into the lonely countryside. For several days he wandered aimlessly, seeing nothing, heading nowhere, his thoughts turned inward to his unhappy failure. But it was spring and no one who has ever worked the land can long ignore the signs this season brings. Sweet promising smells hung gently in the warm air, and all around the oxlips, daisies and celandine splashed the fields in lively yellow. A graceful bird and then another caught Alberic's eye. The busy buzz and click of smaller things were reassuring to his ear and even the bullfrogs' heavy thump set his heart beating once again. His spirits and then his hope revived. The world seemed large and inviting once again.

"There are other places and other things to learn," he thought. "Beauty isn't everything. The true measure of wisdom is utility. I'll do something useful." He hurried now and before long came to a city whose stonecutters and masons were renowned throughout the world for the excellence of their work. His thoughts turned to castles and cloisters, massive walls, towering vaults and steeples which only miracles of skill could hold suspended in the air.

"Everything of use and value is made of stone," he concluded and rushed to seek employment with the master stonecutter.

And for two more years he busied himself learning the secrets of this new vocation— selecting and cutting only the finest stone from the quarry—matching, marking and extracting the giant blocks to be moved on heavy wheeled carts to each new building— and then noting carefully how each shaped stone was fitted in its place so that walls and buttresses grew and arches sprang from pier to pier with such precision that no blade however sharp could slip between the joints. Soon he learned to mix and measure mortar and operate the windlasses whose ingenious ropes and pulleys allowed one man to lift for fifty. Then to make his first careful cuts with bolster and chisel and then stop and watch again as surer hands than his cut and shaped the graceful moldings and intricate tracery which brought the stone to life. As he worked he questioned and remembered everything he saw and heard, and as each day passed, his confidence and his knowledge grew and he began to think of his future life as a great and skillful stonecutter.

When the time came for him to prove his skill to the masons and sculptors of the guild, Alberic chose a piece of specially fine, delicately veined marble and set to work. It was to be the finest carving they had ever seen. With great care he studied and restudied the block and planned his form, then cut into the stone in search of it. He worked in a fever of excitement, his sharp chisels biting off the unwanted material in large chips and pieces. But the image he saw so clearly in his mind seemed always to be just out of sight, a little deeper in the stone. The block grew smaller and the mound of dust and chips larger, and still, like a phantom, the form seemed to recede and still he chased it. Soon there was nothing left at all. The great block of stone had disappeared and soon afterwards, the stonecutter too. For again, without a word, Alberic gathered up his belongings and passed through the city gate. He had failed once more.

"Usefulness isn't everything," he decided after roaming about disconsolately for several days. "Innovation is surely a measure of wisdom. I'll do something original."

The opportunity presented itself in the very next town, where the goldsmiths, it was said, produced objects of unsurpassed excellence and fancy. Bowls and magic boxes, mirrors, shields and scepters, crowns, rings, enchanted buckles and clasps, and candlesticks and vases of incredible grace and intricacy spilled from these workshops and found their way to every royal court and market in the land. It was here that Alberic learned to draw and shape the fine gold wire and work the thin sheets of metal into patterns and textures of light and shape and then inlay these with delicate enamels and precious stones. It was here also that he worked and hoped for the next two years of his life and it was here that for the third time he failed and for the third time took his disappointment to the lonely countryside.

And so it went, from town to town, from city to city, each noted for its own particular craft or enterprise. There were potters who turned and shaped their wet clay into graceful bowls and tall jugs fire-glazed with brilliant cobalt, manganese and copper oxides. Leather finishers who transformed smooth soft skins into shoes and boots, gloves, tunics, bombards, bottles and buckets. There were weavers and spinners who worked in wools and silks, carpenters and cabinetmakers, glassblowers, armorers and tinkers. There were scholars who spent their days searching out the secrets of ancient books, and chemists and physicians, and astronomers determining the precise distances between places that no one had ever seen. And busy ports which offered men the sea and all it touched, and smiths and scribes and makers of fine musical instruments, for anyone with such a bent. Alberic tried them all—and watched and learned and practiced and failed and then moved on again. Yet he kept searching and searching for the one thing that he could do, the secret of the wisdom and skill he so desired.

The years passed and still he traveled on—along the roads and trails and half-forgotten paths—across plains and deserts and forests whose tangled growth held terrors that were sometimes real and sometimes even worse—over hills and cruel high mountain passes and down again perhaps along some unnamed sea—until at last, alone and old and tired, he reached the ramparts of the great capital city.

"I will never find wisdom," he sighed. "I'm a failure at everything."

At the edge of the market square Alberic set his bundle down and watched longingly as all the students, artisans and craftsmen went unconcernedly about their business. He wiped the dust from his eyes and sat for a moment, thinking of his future and his past. What a strange sight he was! His beard was now quite long and grey and the cloak and hat and shoes bore evidence of some repair from every place he'd been. His great bundle bulged with the debris of a lifetime's memories and disappointments and his face was a sad scramble of much the same. As he rummaged through his thoughts, a group of children, struck by his uncommon look, stopped and gathered close around him.

"Where have you come from?"

"What do you do?"

"Tell us what you've seen," they eagerly asked, and poised to listen or flee as his response required.

Alberic was puzzled. What could he tell them? No one had ever sought his conversation before, or asked his opinion on any question. He scratched his head and rubbed his knees, then slowly and hesitantly began to speak, and suddenly the sum of all those experiences, which lay packed up in his mind as in some disordered cupboard, came back to him. He told them of a place or two he'd been and of some lands they'd never known existed and creatures that all their wildest fancies could not invent, and then a story, a legend and three dark mysterious tales remembered from a thousand years before. As he spoke, the words began to come more easily and the pleasure of them eased away his weariness. Everything he'd ever seen or heard or touched or tried was suddenly fresh and clear in his memory, and when the children finally left for home, their faces glowing with excitement, it was to spread the news of the wonderful old man who knew so much.

Since he had no place else to go, Alberic returned to the square each day, and each day the crowds grew larger and larger around him. At first it was only the children, but soon everyone, regardless of age or size, crowded close to listen—and patiently he tried to tell them all they wished to hear. For many of their questions his own experience provided the answers, and for those he could not directly answer he always had a tale or story whose point or artifice led them to answers of their own. More and more he began to enjoy the days and soon he learned to embellish his tales with skillful detail, to pause at just the right time, to raise his voice to a roar or lower it to a whisper as the telling demanded. And the crowds grew even larger.

Workmen came to listen and stayed to learn the secret ways and methods of their own crafts. Artisans consulted him on questions of taste or skill and when they left they always knew more than when they came. Alberic told them everything he had learned or seen through all his failures and his wanderings, and before very long he became known throughout the realm as Alberic the Wise.

His fame spread so far that one day the King himself and several of his ministers came to the square to see for themselves. Cleverly disguised so as not to alert the old man to his purpose, the King posed several questions concerning matters of state and situations in far-off corners of the kingdom. Everything he asked, Alberic answered in great detail, enlarging each reply with accounts of the lore and customs of each region, condition of the crops and royal castles, local problems and controversies, reports on the annual rainfall and the latest depredations by various discontented barons. And for added measure, two songs and a short play (in which he acted all the parts) which he had learned before being dismissed from a traveling theater company.

"You are the wisest man in my kingdom," the astonished King proclaimed, throwing off his disguise, "and you shall have a palace of your own with servants and riches as befits a man of your accomplishments."

Alberic moved into the new palace at once and was more than content with his new life. He enjoyed the wealth and possessions he had never known before, slept on feather beds, ate nothing but the most succulent and delicate foods and endlessly put on and took off the many cloaks, robes and caps the King had graciously provided. His beard was trimmed and curled and he spent his time strolling about the gardens and marble halls posing with proper dignity before each mirror and repeating to himself in various tones and accents, "Alberic the Wise, ALBERIC THE WISE, A-l-b-e-r-i-c T-h-e W-i-s-e!" in order to become accustomed to his new title.

After several weeks, however, the novelty began to wear thin, for a sable cloak is just a sable cloak and a *poulet poêle à l'estragon* is really just another roast chicken. Soon doubts began to crowd out pleasures and by degrees he grew first serious, then sober, then somber and then once again thoroughly discouraged. "How is it possible to be a failure at everything one day and a wise man the next?" he inquired. "Am I not the same person?"

For weeks this question continued to trouble him deeply, and since he could not find a satisfactory answer he returned to the square with his doubts.

"Simply calling someone wise does not make him wise!" he announced to the eager crowd. "So you see, I am not wise." Then, feeling much better, he returned to the palace and began to make ready to leave.

"How modest," the crowd murmured. "The sign of a truly great man." And a delegation of prominent citizens was sent to prevail on him to stay.

Even after listening to their arguments Alberic continued to be troubled and the very next day he returned to the square again.

"Miscellaneous collections of fact and information are not wisdom," he declared fervently. "Therefore I am not wise!" And he returned and ordered workmen to begin boarding up the palace.

"Only the wisest of men would understand this," the people all agreed and petitions were circulated to prevent his leaving.

For several more days he paced the palace corridors unhappily and then returned for a third time.

"A wise man's words are rarely questioned," he counseled gently. "Therefore you must be very careful whom you call wise."

The crowd was so grateful for his timely warning that they cheered for fully fifteen minutes after he had returned to the palace.

Finally, in desperation, he reappeared that very afternoon and stated simply, "For all the years of my life I have sought wisdom and to this day I still do not know even the meaning of the word, or where to find it," and thinking that would convince them he ordered a carriage for six o'clock that afternoon.

The crowd gasped. "No one but a man of the most profound wisdom would ever dare to admit such a thing," they all agreed, and an epic poem was commissioned in his honor.

Once again Alberic returned to the palace. The carriage was canceled, the rooms were opened and aired. There was nothing he could say or do to convince them that he wasn't what they all thought him to be. Soon he refused to answer any more questions or, in fact, to speak at all and everyone agreed that because of the troubled times this was certainly the wisest thing to do. Each day he grew more morose and miserable, and though his fame continued to grow and spread he found no more satisfaction in his success than he had in all his failures. He slept little and ate less and his magnificent robes began to hang like shrouds. The bright optimism that had shone in his eyes through all his travels and hardships began to fade and as the months passed he took to spending all his time at the top of the great north tower, staring without any interest at nothing in particular.

"I am no wiser now than I was before," he said one afternoon, thinking back across the years. "For I still don't know what I am or what I'm looking for." But as he sat there remembering and regretting, he sensed in the air the barest suggestion of some subtle yet familiar scent that drifted in on the freshening breeze. What it was he didn't know—perhaps the pungent tangled aroma of some far eastern bazaar or the sharp and honest smell of a once-known workshop, or it might have been simply the sweet clean air of an upland field the memory of which had long been lost in detail yet retained in some more durable way; but whatever it was it grew stronger and stronger, stirring something deep within him and taking hold of all his thoughts and feelings. His spirit suddenly quickened in response and each breath now came faster than the one before. And then for just a moment he sat quite still—and then at last he knew.

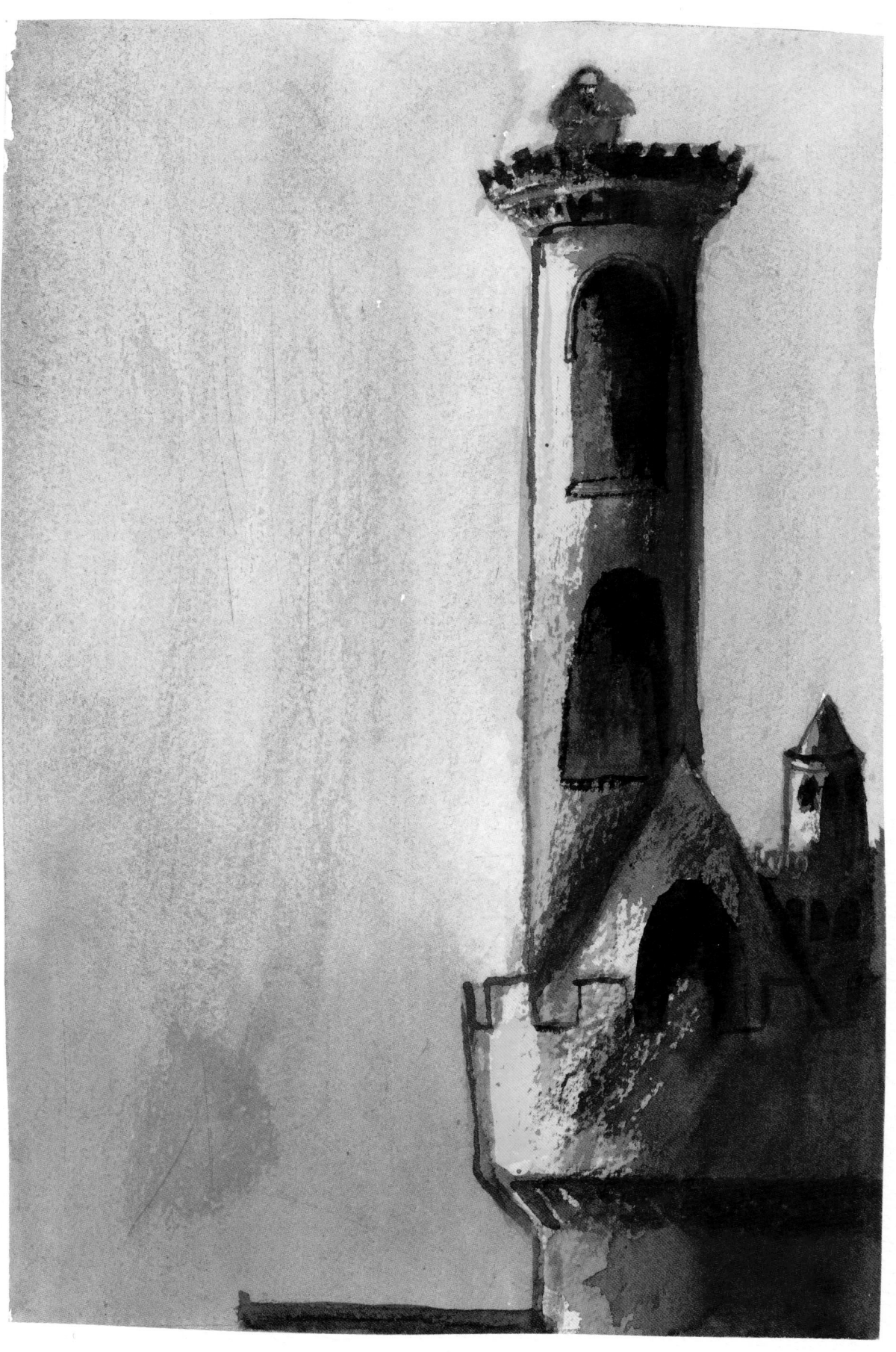

"I am not a glassmaker nor a stonecutter, nor a goldsmith, potter, weaver, tinker, scribe or chef," he shouted happily and he leaped up and bounded down the steep stone stairs. "Nor a vintner, carpenter, physician, armorer, astronomer, baker or boatman." Down and around he ran as fast as he could go, along the palace corridors until he reached the room in which all his old things had been stored. "Nor a blacksmith, merchant, musician or cabinetmaker," he continued as he put on the ragged cloak and shoes and hat. "Nor a wise man or a fool, success or failure, for no one but myself can tell me what I am or what I'm not." And when he'd finished he looked into the mirror and smiled and wondered why it had taken him so long to discover such a simple thing.

So Alberic picked up his bundle, took one last look through the palace and went down to the square for the last time.

"I have at last discovered one thing," he stated simply. "It is much better to look for what I may never find than to find what I do not really want." And with that he said goodbye and left the city as quietly as he'd come.

The crowd gasped and shook their heads in disbelief.

"He has given up his palace!"

"And his wealth and servants!"

"And the King's favor!"

"And he does not even know where he is going," they buzzed and mumbled. "How foolish, how very foolish! How could we ever have thought him wise?" And they all went home.

But Alberic didn't care at all, for now his thoughts were full of all the things he had yet to see and do and all the times he would stop to tell his stories and then move on again. Soon the walls were far behind and only his footsteps and the night were there to keep him company. Once again he felt the freedom and the joy of not knowing where each new step would take him, and as he walked along his stride was longer and stronger than was right somehow for a man his age.